Stuck in the Mud

Jane Clarke

Illustrated by Garry Parsons

Early in the morning,
down on the farm,
a new day was dawning,
peaceful and calm.

The barn door burst open.

"Help! Help!" clucked the hen.

"My poor little **chick!**

He's **stuck** in the **mud** . . .

and the mud's
deep and **thick!**

I've **pushed**

and I've **p u l l e d**

again
and
again . . .

and now
I'm **stuck** too,"
said the poor muddy hen.

Cat heard
the hen.

"Hold on,
wait for me,
it's **purr-fectly** easy,
I'll soon
pull you free."

Cluck!
Cluck!
Cluck!

Cat **pushed** and
she **p u l l e d**
again and again . . .

but soon she was
stuck
with the poor
muddy hen.

Dog heard
the cat.

"I'll help you!"
he yapped.

So he jumped in the mud
and got his paws
trapped.

Dog **pushed** and
he **p u l l e d**
again and again . . .

but soon he was **stuck**
with the cat and the hen.

Sheep heard
the dog . . .

Woof!
Woof!
Woof!

she wasn't thinking,
so she stepped in the mud
and soon
she
was
s i n k i n g.

Sheep **pushed** and she **p u l l e d** again and again . . .

Cheep!

but poor Sheep was **stuck** with Dog, Cat and Hen!

Horse heard
the sheep . . .

Baa!

"Oh neigh!
How **unlucky**,
My horseshoes are sinking,
My tail's getting mucky!"

Horse **pushed** and
he **p u l l e d**
again and again . . .

but then **he was stuck**
with Sheep, Dog, Cat and Hen.

"What's this?"
said the farmer.
"Pooh . . .

this mud is smelly!
And now mucky mud

is all over my wellies!"

He **pushed** and he *p u l l e d* again and again . . .

. . . but the farmer
was **stuck**
with them all,
like the hen.

"Oh dear,"
said the chick . . .

SPLAT!
went the mud as his
little wings flapped.

"It's time I got out."
And with a small p l o p,
Chick jumped off the mud
with a s k i p and a h o p.

"You *pushed* and you **p u l l e d** again and again . . .

but I'm not stuck now and I wasn't stuck then!

"Mud is great fun!
I'm sure you'll agree,
I love mucky mud,

Thanks for playing with me!"